Natural Nia

A Young-Adult Novella

La Rhonda Crosby-Johnson

Author's Note: This is a work of fiction. Names, characters, places, and incidents are a product of the author's imagination. Locales and public names are sometimes used for atmospheric purposes. Any resemblance to actual people, living or dead, or to businesses, companies, events, institutions, or locales is completely coincidental.

Natural Nia/La Rhonda Crosby-Johnson—First Edition

Ordering Information:
For information about bulk purchases, please contact La Rhonda Crosby-Johnson at larhondawrites@gmail.com.

Tradeback ISBN: 979-8-9851228-0-0
eBook ISBN: 979-8-9851228-1-7

Printed in the United States of America

Acknowledgements

There is not enough room here to express sufficient thanks to all the folks who made this work possible. If you read any of the earlier drafts—THANK YOU. If you waited patiently for me to finish "just one more page" so you could then have my full attention—THANK YOU.

If you thought I could do this when I wasn't so sure—THANK YOU. If you said a prayer, uttered an encouraging word, or firmly urged me to get this story finished—THANK YOU.

I want to give a VERY SPECIAL THANK YOU to the creator of this magnificent cover, Dionne Carter (Dionne Nicole Arts). You captured my heart's idea!

And most of all, if you are holding *Natural Nia* in your hands—THANK YOU.

La Rhonda Crosby-Johnson
November 26, 2018

"You have to act as if it were possible to
radically transform the world.
And you have to do it all the time."—
Angela Davis

"Our grandfathers had to run, run, run. My
generation's out of breath.
We ain't running no more."
—Stokely Carmichael (Kwame Ture)

"The revolution has always been in the
hands of the young.
The young always inherit the revolution."
—Huey P. Newton

Also by La Rhonda Crosby-Johnson

Fiction

The Jubilee Taylor Series
A Name That Sang
Buttermilk and Baseball
At Last: Jubilee's Song

Unveiled

Non-fiction/Essays

"Until Jesus Comes Back"
From the anthology *Life's Spices From
Seasoned Sistahs*

"Polka-Dots and Lipstick"
From the anthology *More of Life's Spices:
Seasoned Sistahs Keepin' It Real*

"Dear Michelle"
From the anthology *Go, Tell Michelle: African
American Women Write to the New First Lady*

"Why We 40-ish Sistahs Welcome the Fifties
With Open Arms"
From the anthology *Savvy, Sassy and Bold After
50! A Midlife Rebirth*

"From Negro to Black"
From the anthology *All The Women In My
Family Sing*

For

Karyn Denise Smith

Prologue

The projection screen turned that beautiful blue that always reminded me of the rooftops in Santorini, Greece. The final credits of Spike Lee's documentary *4 Little Girls* about the 1963 bombing of the 16th Street Baptist Church in Birmingham, Alabama had finished. I remembered my father showing me pictures of the four little girls—Addie Mae Collins, Carol Denise McNair, Carole Rosamond Robertson, and Cynthia Wesley—who had been killed in their Sunday school class that day. They had names like my friends and wore the same church shoes and hair ribbons as I had as a girl. Daddy was adamant in making sure I

'understood my history' as he would say.

Angelo Marquez had failed to jump to his

feet to turn off the equipment and turn on

the lights. He liked to call himself our class

audio-visual and lighting technician. Angelo

had a way of making everything he did

sound important.

I was surprised by the silence and

stillness in my usually over-active fifth

period American History class and remained

seated in the back of the room. Cleveland

Preparatory Technical School's Room 125

had a reputation for being loud. I'd received

more than a few calls, on the classroom

phone, from the main office at the opposite

end of the hall to 'keep it down'. The

school's secretary had even demanded we be

quiet once on the PA system. This

embarrassed us all to use hushed tones for a

total of eight minutes.

Maybe I'd dozed off during the film,

and someone had replaced my thirty-seven

eleventh graders with a less rambunctious

group. They'd all moaned and groaned last

week when I started the module on the Civil

Rights Movement. A few had campaigned to

show a film featuring Tyler Perry's

interpretation of a Black matriarch in its

place citing the film's cultural relevance in

2009. I couldn't blame them for trying. In

my twenty-two years of teaching, students

always tried; and I always got them to come

around by infusing my classes with open

and honest dialogue, film, and music. Some

might call me a history nerd. I liked to think

of myself as a passionate history enthusiast.

It was this passion that kept all thirty-seven

desks in my classroom full, while Cleveland

Prep's other two history teachers often

recorded 'cuts' from their classes. My

students moaned and groaned, but they

came. I'd take that over an absence any day.

Che'reese Miller, whose sapphire

nose ring in her right nostril caught the light

from the overhead florescent lights, raised

her hand. "Why didn't somebody do

something? Dang, they were just little girls."

The class came to life with Che'reese's question. Now I recognized them. Game on.

"It was 1963. What do you think they could've done?" Darius Washington fired back at Che'reese. Darius' mother was the head of the Black Studies Department at a local community college. This gave him a better understanding on the turbulence of the 1960s than most of his peers. "They would've just bombed something else. Maybe somebody's house."

"Don't matter what they woulda done, or what we do no way," Michael Davis said in a voice that brought an immediate hush over the room and even caught me off guard. Michael never spoke in class. EVER. "Look at what just happened in Oakland. The police shot a brother who was handcuffed and on the ground. All he was trying to do was catch a train home after a party."

I sighed along with my other students remembering the images that had kept us all glued to our TV sets over the winter break. Oscar Grant, a twenty-two-year-old Black man and father, had been murdered by a BART police officer on New Year's Day. I'd made room in my classes for over a week for students to talk about their feelings and often opened my door at lunchtime to allow students to sit and be together.

"Ms. Graves, Michael's right," Talisha Hopkins declared while using her hands as she always did to make her point. "They keep killing us, and we keep doing nothing." Talisha had transferred to Cleveland Prep mid-semester in the tenth grade. Her family had moved from Detroit after her uncle had been killed by police when he exited a 24 Hour Fitness around three in the morning. The police officer said he'd seen a gun and had feared for his life. The 'gun' turned out to be a black plastic water bottle. Her uncle was still listening to his workout music playing in his headphones and hadn't seen the plainclothes officer or heard the officer's command to 'drop it'.

"Okay. Hold on everybody. Somebody did do something. A lot of somebodies," I said as I walked toward the front of the room and took a seat on my stool. It was painted with swirls of red, black, and green. It had been a gift from my big sister Nia to commemorate my first year of teaching at Cleveland Prep. "Actually, most of the somebodies who have worked on behalf of Black and other oppressed people were and/or are students. Just…Like…You. Some students who once turned this world upside down sat in this very classroom.

"Did you know any of those students, Ms. Graves?" Che'Reese asked. Her eyebrow arched in disbelief. "Students at Cleveland Prep?" Angelo asked with widened eyes.

"The answer to both of your questions is yes," I responded. I glanced at the clock and noticed I'd have just enough time. "Let me tell you all a story."

I

This is a story about hair. You probably find it hard to believe that a hairstyle can change the world, or at least 'the world' of my family, but it did.

It was a bright, sunny morning—the kind that usually made my mother very happy. I think I can even remember her humming some happy little tune…then my sixteen-year-old sister, Sophie, walked into the kitchen. Her once perfectly pressed and curled shoulder-length hair now made a woolly halo around her head. The color drained from my mother's face as she gasped, and the air I was trying to breathe

was taken right out of the room.

"My name is Nia. I will no longer

answer to the name Sophie," my sister said

with her back straight, arms at her sides. She

looked my mother straight in the eyes,

placed her school books on the table, like

she did every morning, and went to the

refrigerator for the carton of milk.

My nine-year-old brother, Lester,

lifted his right fist in the air, his left still

clutched a cornflake-laden spoon, and said,

"Right On, Black Sister."

My maternal grandmother, Annie

Jean Taylor, popped him on the back of the

head to quiet him. I sat starring at my sister

with my stomach doing somersaults.

Mama's breathing returned to

normal, and she found her voice. "Whoever

you are. March yourself upstairs and get

ready for school."

"Mama, I am ready," Sophie

declared. She poured milk on her cornflakes.

"If you mean get my hair ready, it is.

Naturally ready."

Before Mama could say the next

thing that was fighting to burst from

between her full, beautiful lips, Gran spoke

in her firm, quiet voice, "Make sure your

brother gets to the library after school to get

that book on alligators he needs for his book report."

Sophie nodded and looked over at Lester with a smile and a quick wink.

I'd forgotten my mouth was full of orange juice until it flew open, and the juice splashed all over the front of my dress.

"Arnetta, look at the mess you're making," Mama snapped. She reached for a towel to wipe up the juice that had spilled onto the table before it reached her always just-mopped linoleum floor. She gave Sophie a look that said, 'this is all your fault'."

"Arnetta, get cleaned up now; or you'll be late for school," Gran said as she added Carnation Half & Half to her coffee.

"Mama, can I get me a natural like….like…," Lester paused and whispered to Sophie, "What you say your name is now?"

"Nia, Little Brother," she said and smiled at him, then took a sip from her glass filled with orange juice.

"Mama, can I get me a natural like Nia?" Lester asked. His face turned into one great, big toothy grin.

"You can get up from my table and get ready for school, Lester Anthony Graves," Mama snapped again using all of his names and walked toward the sink with a

dish towel full of orange juice.

"Have a nice day, Mama," Sophie

said while she gathered her books and left

the kitchen as if she hadn't turned the day

upside down. I'd had enough of this day

already and hurried from the kitchen to

change my dress and leave for school.

"Arnetta, give your mother a chance

to get used to it before you go working

yourself into a fit," Gran advised as she

waved goodbye to Lester. He leaped up the front steps of Jefferson Elementary School.

"What do you think has gotten into Sophie?" I asked as we continued our walk to Washington Junior High School. I was a seventh grader there, and Gran worked in the cafeteria. Usually, I walked to school with my three best friends in the world: Stacy Jones, Denise Hughes, and Carol Robinson. Today was not a 'usual' day, so I'd sent Stacy, Denise, and Carol ahead without me and decided to walk with Gran so we could talk.

"Honey, she's becoming a woman and trying to make sense of a world that's changing. She's trying to find her place in it. Like I did. Like your mama did. Like

you'll do one day." Gran smiled and patted

my shoulder in the way that usually

reassured me. Today, it did nothing to help

settle the uneasy feeling in the pit of my

stomach. "And she wants to be called Nia."

"Where'd she get that name?" I

asked frowning. It sounded strange to my

ears. I couldn't imagine it coming out of my

mouth. "What does it mean anyway?"

"You'll have to ask her, Arnetta. I'm

not sure," Gran said as we neared the school.

"Try to get your mind back on your business

and leave your sister to hers."

As my grandmother walked toward

the door marked CAFETERIA

EMPLOYEES and I raced toward the yard

to meet my best friends, I doubted if I'd ever

be able to return to 'my business' again.

II

"You think your mama's gonna let her keep her hair that way?" Carol asked as she stuffed an OREO cookie into her mouth at lunch. The thought made my head swim.

"Lester, with his crazy, old self, asked my mama if he could get a natural." I had finally found something in this terrible day that made me laugh. "He's even calling her by her new name."

"I think it's kind of cool," Denise said, then sipped from her milk carton. "I think I'll get one when I get to Cleveland Prep."

"One what? A new name or a natural?" Carol asked.

"Maybe both," Denise answered. She drained the milk carton with a slurp that would've gotten any one of us sent to our room from our dinner tables.

"Are you CRAZY?!" I gasped and looked at Denise, my best friend since kindergarten, as if I'd never seen her before. "Why would you want all that nappy hair on your head, Denise? Don't be ridiculous."

"Dang, Arnetta. Calm down before you pop a gut or something." Stacy laughed. "She was only teasing."

"Well it's not funny. This is serious, you guys," I said sighing. Denise handed her apple to me and I handed her my pear.

Momentarily, the world was back to normal.

Sitting in the kitchen doing my homework that evening, I wondered how many more changes my life could stand. After all, I was only twelve years old. I was certain that was not old enough to handle too many changes. I was ten when the biggest change in my life happened, and I was just now getting used to it. Thinking back on it, that winter holiday may have been the saddest time of my life.

Daddy had moved out of our house. I couldn't believe it. It was the day after New Year's Day; a time when every day was fun, because there was no school. Mama let us stay up late because Aunt Teresa came to visit. We'd had the best Christmas ever. Daddy had played Santa Claus at the church's annual Christmas Eve party just like always. That night after we'd taken our baths, put on our pajamas, and left cookies and milk for Santa, Daddy had let me and Lester sit on his lap while he read, **Twas the Night Before Christmas**. *He'd kissed Mama under the mistletoe as Lester made gagging noises, I giggled, and Sophie looked on in* *her new grown-up way that said she understood everything. The gifts under the tree on Christmas morning let us know Santa had read the fine print on our Christmas letters: a new bike for me and outfits for my Barbie, a new baseball and baseball mitt for Lester, and a new record player for Sophie.*

On New Year's Day, Daddy and Gran had sprawled out in the den after eating too much of Mama's traditional New Year's Day dinner of chitterlings, greens, and black-eyed peas. They fought over the football game and ate sweet potato pie and peach cobbler. Sophie let me hear her new

Stevie Wonder album, and Aunt Teresa

showed Lester how to throw a real spitball.

"Ain't we going to wait for Daddy?"

I asked as we sat down to dinner the next

day—January 2. I should have known

something was wrong when Mama didn't

correct my 'ain't' to 'aren't'. Instead she

rushed from the table; Aunt Teresa followed

closely behind her. I heard Mama crying

before her bedroom door closed.

"Your father won't be living here

anymore," Gran said calmly. She paused to

let her words land softly. "He's left your

mother."

"Why?" I asked. My throat was so

dry that the words came creaking out like a

door swinging on rusty hinges. "Doesn't he love us anymore?"

"Arnetta, you'll have to ask your father about his reasons. Although I'm sure his leaving has nothing to do with him not loving y'all." Gran's voice was soft as she handed me the handkerchief she always had in her dress pocket. I hadn't felt the tears streaming down my face until that moment.

"Are they getting a divorce?" Sophie asked. Lester was busy forking collard greens into his mouth and wasn't paying much attention to us. The word 'divorce' hung in the air like icicles.

"I don't know that, Sophie," Gran answered. "When things settle down, I'm sure your parents will explain it all to you."

"I don't want anything explained to me! I want things the way they were yesterday! The way they are supposed to be! I want my Daddy back home, NOW!" I screamed running away from the table.

It was two days later when Mama could stop crying for longer than ten minutes at a time. She sat us all down in the living room to explain. Daddy had moved across town where we'd lived until Lester was born, and Mama had finished going to college to become a social worker. He was staying with his older brother Eddie Graves,

Sr. and his brother's wife, Ruthie. This was all the explaining Mama could manage before the tears started again. She left the room to lie down. Gran went into the kitchen to start dinner. Sophie took Lester outside to play catch with the new baseball mitt and baseball Daddy had given him for Christmas. I sat on the sofa, my bare legs sticking to the hard plastic that covered it, looking at the photographs of my parents on the mantel. My eyes seemed unable to move from the photograph of them smiling in their smart navy blue wedding suits. Mama had rice stuck in the soft curls on top of her head, and Daddy looked so handsome. I cried hard, because my family as I had

known it was no more.

    Snapping back to the present, I
began to focus again on my algebra. After I
finished my homework, I grabbed my book
and other belongings from the kitchen table.
While I walked up the stairs to my room, I
had a feeling more changes were coming.

III

"Brenda, Brenda. You gone have to lower your voice and slow down," Leon said firmly as his ex-wife screeched. He noticed the glances from the other men in the garage before he was able to guide her into his office and close the door. He moved some boxes containing oil filters from a chair in front of his desk and asked her to sit down.

"Sit down! Sit down! Leon is that your only answer to this mess? Sit down!" Brenda yelled. Her words could surely be heard through the closed door. Leon doubted anyone was getting any work done. "Your daughter has lost her mind and gotten mixed up with some nappy-headed hoodlums, and all you can think to say to me is 'sit down'." Brenda paced the small office like a caged animal.

Leon sighed as he leaned against the desk. He didn't need Brenda nor her hysterics today. He was short two men, had payroll to finish, and was a day behind on rebuilding a carburetor. "Brenda, what do you want me to do?"

"Do I have to figure out everything, always?" Brenda yelled. She stopped her pacing to place her right hand on her hip and glare at him. "Or, did you divorce yourself from your ability to problem-solve when you divorced me?"

Leon glanced at the clock on the wall behind Brenda's head and decided to ignore the question altogether. There would never be enough time to explain.

"Brenda, I just think you're making this thing bigger than it is," Leon said trying to remain calm. "She's just expressing herself like teenagers do."

"Expressing herself? Expressing herself? Do you ever take your head from under the hood of a car long enough to read the newspapers?" Brenda asked. She looked at him as if he had just grown an eye in the middle of his forehead. "Sophie is caught up in the midst of some anti-government 'Black Power Movement' or something. She's put her hair into one of those God-awful, wild naturals and wants us to call her Nia for Christ's sake. What kind of name is that?"

"It's KiSwahili," Leon said. He hoped the smile he felt on the inside had not made it to his face. He had taught Sophie the Nguzo Saba when she was a small girl. She had not forgotten."It means 'purpose'."

"Leon Graves, are you in on this with her? Are you the one filling her head with a lot of that old African nonsense you were so fond of before you dropped out of college? Leon, are you working against me?" Brenda asked as the bitter taste of anger mixed with the saliva in her mouth.

Leon forced himself to take a deep breath. He would not allow Brenda to suck him into another fight over the kids. "I just don't think it's something to get all worked up about. Kids are taking a stand. They trying to make changes we couldn't make. I just don't think it's all that bad, is all I'm saying."

He took another breath and tried to push Brenda's comment about dropping out of college out of his head. She had gotten pregnant. His father told him that a man takes responsibility for his actions, so he married her. It wasn't as if he didn't love her. He had loved Brenda Taylor since the first time he'd seen her at a Sunday school convention. It was just that he had some other things he had wanted to do before he became a husband and a father. He married Brenda and left school to work full time. He had never regretted his decision; but every time she mentioned it, it always sounded like he had been some irresponsible bum dropping out of school to mess around.

"Leon Graves. That is the most ridiculous thing I have heard you say in a long, long time. I see you are not going to be of any help in this situation. Thanks for nothing, Leon!" Brenda yelled and snatched open the office door. She stormed out of the garage.

Leon wondered if 10:30 in the

morning was too early for a beer.

IV

On the first and third Saturday of each month, for as long as I could remember, Mama, Sophie, and I drove downtown to *Rena's House of Beauty* to get our hair washed, pressed, and curled. Sometimes to save on money, Mama would wash my hair first and just pay for the press and curl part. I hated the trips to *Rena's House of Beauty*. I always left the salon with the top of at least one ear burned from the hot comb or curling iron. Mama said it was my fault for squirming. I thought it was because I had to be still for too long in a hot room and sit on a phone book placed on a chair that was built for grown-ups and not kids. With the way things had been going at my house since Sophie's new hairdo and name, I thought maybe doing something we'd done forever would return my family to normal. I was actually looking forward to this Saturday's visit. Was I wrong.

"Mama says come on," I yelled up the stairs to my sister. I still refused to use her new name, so I avoided using any name at all.

"Tell Mama to go ahead," she said walking calmly into the kitchen and bringing that 'natural' with her. "I won't be going to Rena's anymore. Her idea of beauty is no longer mine."

"Sophie, can you just stop all this and come on?" I pleaded and forgot not to call her Sophie. "Mama's already in the car, and you know she's going to have a fit if you make us late."

She ignored me and turned on the radio. My favorite Jackson 5 song, "The Love You Save" burst into the kitchen. I had what Daddy called a 'terminal' crush on Michael Jackson, but not even hearing Michael's voice could make things better.

"Mama! Mama!" I called opening the kitchen screen door and yelling toward the driveway where Mama sat in the idling car. "She says she's not coming."

"I am losing my patience with Sophie and her nonsense," Mama mumbled as she opened the car door, came up the back steps, and pushed past me into the kitchen. "Sophie Leona Graves, get your narrow behind in the car. I have had enough of your little 'Black Power' experiment. We have an appointment at Rena's in twenty minutes, and I intend for us to be there. All of us. Now get in the car!"

Sophie just looked at Mama with a sad look, opened the refrigerator, and took out a carton of chocolate milk. I couldn't believe it. Nobody ever, ever ignored Mama like that. I closed my eyes, sure that I'd hear Sophie yell when Mama landed the belt (that always miraculously appeared at times like this) on her behind. There was no yell. Maybe Mama had killed her without making a single sound. I opened one eye.

"Mama, try calling her Nia," I whispered from the safety of the corner.

"Arnetta, shut up and go get in the car!" Mama yelled at me.

I felt like I had just been slapped. Mama never told any of us to 'shut up'. Those two words were forbidden in our house and on the 'bad words' list right along with the words beginning with 'a', 'd', and 'sh'. I made my way quickly toward the back door. I was careful not to let the screen door slam behind me. If Mama was going to kill my sister, I did not want to have to

testify that I had seen it. I stood on the back

porch listening instead.

"I am going to say this one more

time, Sophie," Mama dragged her name out

before taking a deep breath. I heard the heels

of her shoes crossing the kitchen floor. "I

have had enough of your nonsense and your

nappy head. I want you to go get in the car

with your sister right now."

"Mama, I'm sorry you are so upset;

but, this is not about you. This is about me.

Who I am and the kind of woman I want to

be." Sophie was not backing down, and I

wondered if they could make you testify if

you only *heard* your mother kill your sister.

"Brenda, take Arnetta and go on to Rena's before you make yourself late." I breathed a sigh of relief as I heard Gran's voice. Mama would never kill her own daughter in front of *her* own mother.

I heard Mama's feet coming toward the back door and ran to get in the car before she caught me on the back porch. I had just climbed onto the backseat and left the door open so it would not make any noise closing when I saw Mama come down the back steps. Defeat was in her every step.

The ride to *Rena's House of Beauty,* which was usually filled with laughter and music from the radio that Mama always let me and Sophie turn up loud, was silent. I amused myself on the backseat with a book

Lester had left on there about sled dogs and

tried to hear music in my head.

As much as I dreaded Miss Rena's

hot comb, I was glad it would not be in

Mama's hand. Today, I would have

probably had both my ears burned right off

the sides of my head.

Since Daddy had moved out of the

house, press-and-curl Saturday now

included Mama dropping me and Sophie off

at Daddy's garage for our weekend visit.

Daddy always came to pick up Lester early

on our press-and-curl Saturdays so he could

take Lester to the barbershop with him. As

usual, Daddy was standing outside when

Mama pulled up at two o'clock in the afternoon. Lester was running around chasing a brown and white puppy that Mama probably said had mange. She kissed me on the forehead and reminded me not to mess up my hair. She waved to Lester, who now held the puppy in his arms, and pulled away from the curb. She did not even glance at Daddy, although he waved. He always waved at her retreating car the first and third Saturday of each month.

"Hey, Nettie-girl," Daddy said and smiled while playfully attempting to pull at one of the Shirley Temple curls hanging from my ponytails that were adorned with ribbons. I ducked, saving my ponytails, as he laughed. "Give me a couple of minutes to clean up, and we'll head on out of here."

I got a bottle of Coca-Cola from the ice chest Daddy kept just inside the garage door, sat down on an old bench, and watched Lester try to teach his puppy to fetch a stick. Since Daddy didn't ask where Sophie was, I figured she must have already called him and told him what happened. I wondered where she was. Maybe she was already at Uncle Eddie's waiting for us.

The Coca-Cola and watching Lester, with his crazy self, do more stick-fetching than the puppy he'd named Lucky helped me forget about my sister almost getting killed in the kitchen this morning and the look in Mama's eyes when we walked into

Rena's House of Beauty without Sophie.

Just as Daddy came out of the garage and

called to Lester, a blue pickup truck drove

up and pulled into the driveway. Sophie was

in the cab of the truck with a boy I'd never

seen before. His natural was bigger than

hers, and I wondered how they fit all that

nappy hair into such a small space.

"Daddy, I want you to meet my

friend Jamal Robinson." Sophie smiled and

took 'The Natural's' hand as they walked

toward Daddy. "Jamal, this is my father,

Leon Graves."

"Nice to meet you, sir," Jamal said

holding out his hand.

"Likewise," Daddy said and shook Jamal's hand. Daddy always used the 'Black handshake'. Mama threatened to break both of our arms if she ever saw any of us kids shaking hands like that. She called it 'mess' except she put the word in front of it that white people used sometimes when they were being mean and nasty to Black people.

"That's my sister, Arnetta," Sophie said and nodded in my direction. She acted as if the thought gave her a headache. "I have a little brother named Lester around here somewhere."

"Hey, Little Sister," Jamal said and flashed a smile that under different circumstances would've probably made me giggle.

"I am not your *sister*," I said doing my best imitation of the voice Mama used whenever a man yelled 'Hey, foxy lady' as she walked by. "I am not even sure if I am still HER sister." I stomped away to find Lester and Lucky.

"Ignore her. She's twelve," Sophie explained with that grown-up sounding voice that made me sick to my stomach.

"I heard that, Sophie!" I called back over my shoulder as I ran around the side of the garage. I made sure to yell the name she now hated.

"Daddy, would it be all right if I meet you in a couple of hours? There's a meeting at the community center, and I really want to go," Sophie asked.

"What kind of meeting?" Daddy asked. He gave Jamal a look that brought the temperature of the warm afternoon down at least ten degrees.

"It's about renaming the community center, the Malcolm X Community Center. There's going to be a lecture on Black Nationalism and the need for economic development in the Black community," Jamal said and met Daddy's eyes. "I'll have her home by seven, sir."

"You'll have her home by six, Jamal. Wait for my daughter in the truck, would you?" Daddy shook Jamal's hand again and walked back toward the garage with his arm around Sophie's shoulders. "He a student at Cleveland Prep?"

"No, Daddy. He graduated from Roosevelt High School last year," Sophie explained. "He's eighteen and works at the Black Bugle, the Black Liberation newspaper. He takes a couple of sociology classes at the community college and works as an orderly at the county hospital. He wants to be a journalist one day. Daddy, please say I can go. Please."

"Go on to your meeting. And no matter what you call yourself, remember you still my little girl. Make sure 'Jamal-The-Wonderful' knows that too." Leon smiled as she quickly hugged him and ran toward the truck before he could change his mind. Leon waved as the truck pulled out of the driveway and headed back toward the garage to find his two younger children.

V

I loved my weekends with Daddy.

He lived at Uncle Eddie's house over the

garage in a little apartment he'd fixed up. It

was nothing like our house and that made it

fun. It was crowded and none of the

furniture matched. There wasn't anything in

the house that would cause Daddy to have a

fit if I or Lester knocked it over. Sophie and

I always slept on the sofa bed in the small

living room (which became the dining room

when we brought the TV trays from behind

the refrigerator). Daddy bought twin beds to

put in the apartment's only real bedroom, so

he and Lester could sleep in there. Aunt

Ruthie always asked if we wanted to sleep in the house because there was more room, but we always said no. It was kind of fun being crowded close together. It made up for us being so far away from Daddy all those days in between our visits.

I thought I'd finally get some peace and quiet and could concentrate on just having fun and not having to think about Sophie's nappy head at Daddy's place. Maybe the world would return to normal here on Aunt Ruthie's back steps. No such luck.

"You think Sophie gonna run off with the Black Panthers?" asked my eleven-year-old cousin Rachel as she balanced a paper plate filled with fried chicken and baked beans on her skinny knees.

"The Panthers is what's happenin'," Eddie, Jr., who we called June, said. He did his best to make his squeaky thirteen-year-old voice sound cool like the boys in high school. "Mama let me buy a poster of Huey Newton. He's their leader. It's up in my room. You want to see it, Arnetta?"

I had absolutely no idea what either one of them was talking about, but even as mad as I'd been with Sophie lately, I didn't want her running off with panthers. After all, she was my *sister*; my *only* sister Mama always said when she wanted us to get along. I took another bite from the crispy drumstick and hunched my shoulders. Sophie didn't even like cats, so I doubted she'd run off with any panthers. As I filled my mouth with the cinnamon-sweet flavor of Aunt Ruthie's baked beans, I wondered if June was sniffing glue or something. My friend Stacy said her thirteen-year-old cousin from Detroit was sniffing glue and talking crazy. June talking about Sophie running off with panthers sounded glue-sniffing crazy to me.

"Her name ain't Sophie no more. It's Nia," said Lester proudly. His lips and chin were greasy from the fried chicken. "It means purpose."

"Solid," June said. He attacked a chicken wing with his two front teeth that always reminded me of a chipmunk.

"June, what's so 'solid' about Sophie running around looking like some wild woman with a head full of nappy hair? She got Mama screaming and telling people to 'shut up'. Instead of being out here with us, she's gone to some meeting with some old nappy-headed boy with a name he probably made up one morning. I don't see nothing so 'solid' about that," I said finishing my drumstick and chewing as if that would turn my upside-down life right-side up again.

"June, ain't Sophie scared them panthers will bite her?" asked my nine-year-old cousin David whose mouth was full of baked beans.

"They ain't no real panthers, stupid. It's the name of the group. The panther is a symbol of power. Black Power. Whitey see that black panther, he know we ain't taking none of his jive," June explained. He waved his chicken wing for emphasis. I rolled my eyes at him wondering when he started talking like he was raised by wolves. He pretended not to see me and continued. "Me and Howard been reading all about them over at the community center. We thinking about writing Comrade Huey and starting a Junior Panther chapter right here."

"June, have you lost your mind too? Aunt Ruthie ain't about to let you join a bunch of Negroes who go around calling themselves panthers," I said wishing the subject would change before I lost my appetite. There was lemon Jell-O cake and grape Kool-Aid in the kitchen.

"You just wait and see, Arnetta. You keep talking to me like that and me and Howard ain't gone let you join," June threatened. "What Nia's doing is 'Right On' with me. You ain't got to be so uptight about it. You startin' to act just like Aunt Brenda."

That did it. He'd gone and made me lose my appetite before I had my lemon Jell-O cake, AND now he was talking about my mama. Nobody talked about my mama. My paper plate with the bare drumstick bone and the rest of my baked beans hit the ground as I jumped from the step above June onto his back. We landed at the bottom of the stairs in a heap. By the time Daddy and Uncle Eddie made it to the backyard, we'd been tussling in the dirt for a while.

"What the hell is going on out here?" Uncle Eddie asked. He held June by the collar of his shirt. It was covered in dirt, and I could see a few buttons missing.

"Arnetta went nuts and jumped on my back," June explained looking down at the damage to his shirt and giving me a look that let me know this was only round one.

"Arnetta, we don't fight family," Daddy said with a look of disappointment on his face and a firm hold on my arm.

"He started it," I snapped, too angry to care if my smart mouth would get me Daddy's belt.

"Lord! Look at your head, Arnetta! Brenda would kill me, if she saw your head," Aunt Ruthie said opening the back door. My five year-old cousin Joseph slipped past her as she held the door open. "Get on in here and get cleaned up! If I have to do your hair over tonight, you gone break me off a switch."

Rachel, loyal to a fault, followed me and kicked dirt at June in an act of solidarity.

"June, you and David get this mess cleaned up out here," Uncle Eddie said releasing his grip on his oldest son. He shook his head. "Things never change. Do they, Brother?"

"You must be thinking about all those fights you and Lula used to have," Daddy said and laughed.

"*Aunt* Lula?" June asked unable to imagine his always dressed-to-the-nines aunt rolling around in the dirt fighting his father.

"If you think your cousin Arnetta is nuts, you should've seen our little sister in her day. That girl was wild *and* crazy." Uncle Eddie laughed.

"June, your daddy was always saying or doing something to get that girl riled up," Daddy said and shook his head at the memory. Slowly the smile left his face as he thought about what had just happened. "I don't know what got into Arnetta. She knows we don't fight family. I better go talk to her."

"Ruthie will take care of it. Don't worry about it," Uncle Eddie said. "They cousins, Leon. They supposed to fight. Come take a ride with me over to Jack's Place; a cold, tall one will take that worried look off your face."

VI

"That hair of yours sure is causing the family a lot of trouble. I like it though," Aunt Ruthie said as Sophie came down the hallway to the kitchen for breakfast the next morning.

Sophie gave her hair one last pat, stole a look at herself in the large hallway mirror, and entered the kitchen as if she were appearing before her royal subjects. She gave Aunt Ruthie a quick peck on her cheek as her large natural lightly brushed Aunt Ruthie's cheek. She grabbed a buttered hot biscuit from my plate and eased onto her chair next to Daddy. She bit into the biscuit before I had a chance to protest.

"Thanks, Aunt Ruthie. I wish Mama felt the same way," Sophie commented with a pained look on her face. Aunt Ruthie passed her a plate stacked high with crunchy strips of bacon. "She's been on my case about it for the last couple of months."

"Give Brenda a chance, honey," Aunt Ruthie said taking a quick look at Daddy. "She'll come around." For Sophie's sake, Aunt Ruthie made her words sound more hopeful than she felt. She'd known our mother since they were children, and it was more likely Mama would never come around.

"That's what I been trying to tell her," Daddy said and spooned scrambled eggs onto Lester's plate. Sophie gave Daddy that look that said they understood something no one else at the table could understand. I filled the biscuit Sophie had left on my plate with strawberry jam and hoped the conversation would change.

"Baby, it just takes your mama a while to adjust to things changing around her. Try to understand her side of it and don't make it harder than it has to be," Aunt Ruthie urged and then patted Sophie reassuringly on the shoulder.

As if in answer to my prayers, Joseph knocked his milk over and took the attention off Sophie and her stupid hair.

"June, take Joseph upstairs and change his shirt, "Aunt Ruthie said. She wiped up the spilled milk. "And tell your daddy to hurry up. I'd like this family to get to church before the benediction at least one Sunday this month."

VII

"You should have seen all the nappy heads in that place," I said while changing into the red shorts and the yellow and red T-shirt that served as our girl's gym uniform. I was in the middle of reporting on my Sunday at St. Luke AME Church. "Sophie fit right in."

"I heard the new preacher over at the AME on 23rd Avenue got a natural. Instead of a preacher's robe, he wears one of those dashikis and a pair of blue jeans. My mama says it's disgraceful to go to the Lord's house dressed like a heathen," Carol said and took a deep breath as she squeezed her plump thighs into Stacy's extra pair of gym shorts. Carol had left her gym bag again and could not afford another 'out-of-uniform cut'.

"Reverend Lawry at Greater Grace says all this is a trick of the devil to ruin our minds," said Stacy. She applied a generous amount of strawberry lip gloss to her lips, then handed the lip gloss to Denise. "Sophie wants to go there every Sunday. That started fight *Number Seven Hundred and Eleven* this morning. We've gone to St. John forever," I said and wondered if there would ever be a morning in my house again when my mother and sister weren't screaming at each other about something.

"They couldn't have been yelling any louder than Clayton and my daddy all weekend. Clayton told Daddy he wasn't going to college. He's joining the Peace Corps after he graduates and going to Africa," Stacy said.

"I'll just be glad when this mess is all over and things go back to normal." I sighed as we fastened the combination locks on our gym lockers and headed to the field. As I stood on my number for attendance, I wondered if anybody would remember 'normal' when all this was over.

VIII

After a month of 'Nia' and her natural, Mama tried a new tactic to get Sophie to press her hair. Instead of the frontal attack, which always ended with Sophie's hair still nappy, Mama took a sneak approach: her secret weapon—*my* pressed hair.

"Arnetta, baby. Bring me that bag on the chair," Mama said one evening after Walter Cronkite had relayed the nightly news. We were all in the den. Gran was knitting and watching Lester build a castle with his LEGO set. Sophie was reading a book she'd wrapped in a book cover made from a brown paper bag that had the continent of Africa drawn in red, black, and green across the front. I walked over to the chair, picked up the bag, and brought it to Mama.

"Go on and open it," Mama said and nodded her head. She glanced quickly at Sophie.

"Ah, wow!" I exclaimed and carefully took a handful of satin hair ribbons from the bag. There must have been almost twenty ribbons in that bag; their colors spilled over my hand in a vibrant, silky rainbow as I pulled them from the bag. "Thank you, Mama." I gave her a loud kiss on the cheek and hugged her neck tightly.

"I thought they would look very pretty in your hair. The lady at the store said even some of the high school girls are wearing them." Mama looked at Sophie as she spoke. Sophie continued to read her book.

"I've got to call Stacy, Denise, and Carol," I said rushing to the kitchen to use the phone.

"Did you bring me and Nia something, Mama?" Lester asked. He'd been watching the whole thing, his castle momentarily forgotten. Mama never brought just one of us a treat like this.

"Lester, you would look pretty funny in hair ribbons." Mama choked out a laugh with her eyes fixed on Sophie's hair.

"Well, I wouldn't look funny with a new Duncan yo-yo," Lester said hoping Mama had another bag somewhere close. "Would I, Nia?"

For the first time, Sophie lifted her eyes from her book and spoke. "You would look great with a new Duncan yo-yo, Lester." She stood and looked directly at Mama. "Much better than anyone could ever look in hair ribbons." She walked out of the room.

Lester went back to his castle. His attention was now focused on making a draw bridge. Gran looked up from her knitting in time to see Mama bite her lower lip. A sure sign that she was so angry she needed help keeping her mouth shut.

I named the battle taking place between Mama and Sophie 'The Natural Wars'. They were entering their third month. My stomach started to ache each time the two of them were in the same room. Lester started to have nightmares, and I wondered if he dreamed of Sophie's natural. Gran was sure it was because of a Dracula movie he'd confessed to watching with June. I was so angry at Sophie for turning our world upside down that I hardly noticed how proud I was of her for standing her ground with Mama. I was sure Sophie never knew it, and I

certainly would never tell her, but I'd always

sort of looked up to her. I guess that wasn't

too strange since she was my big sister; but I

think even if Sophie had been my little

sister, it would have been hard not to look

up to her. She always seemed to know what

she was doing, and she had ideas and

thoughts about everything. The 'Natural

Wars' were pretty serious though, and it was

certainly safer for me to side with Mama. I

pretended that none of it bothered me, but

most of the time I felt really sad about all the

yelling and screaming. However, there were

a few benefits from 'The Natural Wars' for

me. Mama was trying so hard to make

Sophie jealous that she was going out of her way to be nice to me. She even took me, Stacy, Denise, and Carol to see the Jackson 5 and never complained about the music being too loud or us jumping around and screaming like we were crazy.

Sophie and I hardly ever talked anymore since I refused to call her 'Nia', and she refused to answer when I called her Sophie. Sophie's best friends—Janet Goldsby, Deborah Hayes, and Tanya Adams—all had naturals now. Mama wouldn't let Sophie visit her friends anymore, and they weren't allowed to come to the house. I thought after that, Sophie would get lonely and have to speak to me;

but she didn't and either found something to read or talked to Gran and Lester instead. She only spoke to me when it would have been too rude not to speak.

I told myself that I didn't want or need a sister anymore. When Mama let me go to a sleepover at Denise's one Friday night instead of staying home, I was glad for the break. I wasn't prepared, however, for what I saw. Or should I say, what I didn't see when I came back home late that Saturday afternoon.

"Gran! Gran!" I yelled as I flew down the stairs and into the kitchen. My ponytails, decorated with rainbow ribbons, made a breeze around my head. Gran stood at the stove, her attention on basting a pot

roast. "Call the police! We've been robbed."

"Robbed? Arnetta, what are you

talking about?" Gran asked as she covered

the pot roast and returned it to the oven.

"Sophie's things. They're gone." I

panted, now out of breath from my race to

the kitchen. Why was Gran sitting down at

the table and opening up the newspaper

instead of calling the police from the

kitchen's wall phone? "Gran, they even took

her bed."

"Arnetta Elizabeth Graves," Gran

said lowering the newspaper. She had used

all my names, so I knew she was about to

say something very important. "Listen to

yourself, child. Do you honestly think someone would come into the house, with me in the kitchen, on a Saturday afternoon to steal your sister's bed? Better yet, do you think I'd have sat here while they did?"

"She's in the attic," Lester said in a matter-of-fact way as he walked into the kitchen and took two cookies from the cookie jar. He looked at me as if he wondered how anybody could be so stupid. He even shook his head at me before leaving the kitchen. The kind of head-shaking people do when they see a crazy person digging through a garbage can.

"The attic?" I asked. I was totally confused. "What's she doing in the attic?"

"Go ask her, Arnetta," Gran answered and returned to her newspaper.

I knew Gran was finished with this conversation, so I decided it was time to find out exactly what was going on in this house.

The sound of Marvin Gaye's "What's Going On" met my ears as I opened the attic door and pulled the chain that would light the steep stairway.

"What are you doing up here?" I asked at the top of the stairs. Sophie had turned our junky, dusty, old attic into a bedroom. There were posters of June's "Comrade Huey," his panthers, and a woman with a natural even bigger than

Sophie's covering one wall. Brightly colored fabric covered the remaining walls.

"I was going to ask you the same thing," Sophie said as she looked up from her sewing machine.

"Does Mama know you're up here?" I questioned. Surely, Mama would never have approved of this. "With all your stuff?"

"Arnetta, did you come up here for a reason or just to ask dumb questions?" Sophie asked. She held her sewing creation up and beamed.

"What's that?" I asked.

"It's a dashiki," Sophie answered. Pride in her creation was written all over her face.

"A what?" I asked. I hope she wasn't planning to wear that thing during dinner tonight. It would surely drive Mama the rest of the way to crazy.

"A dashiki, Arnetta. It's an African shirt." Sophie placed the garment on the ironing board that was next to her sewing machine and plugged in the iron.

"Are you going to wear that thing?" I asked. If she said yes, I'd have to find a way to get back over to Denise's for dinner.

"No, Arnetta. This one is worn by men," she answered and tested the heat of the iron with a quick touch of her moistened index finger like Gran always did.

"A man? What man would be caught wearing that thing?" I asked.

Sophie just rolled her eyes at me before she returned her attention to her ironing.

I decided to let Mama handle this when she got home. She and Sophie would need something to argue about tonight and Sophie's dashiki was a good candidate. There were more important things for us to discuss.

"Sophie, are you *really* going to sleep up here all the time?" I placed my right hand on my hip like I'd seen Mama do when she really wanted an answer from one of us.

"Arnetta, if you are going to have a conversation with me, you will use my name. The name I've chosen for myself is Nia, and I'd appreciate your using it when addressing me," she stated. Her attention never left the dashiki.

That was it! "Then you know what? I won't have a conversation with you!" I yelled. I was so angry at her for napping up her hair, changing her name, moving her bed into the attic, and making dashikis for men. "And I won't call you any old stupid name you picked out either. You already have a name: Sophie Leona Graves. That's your name."

"Arnetta, get out of my room," she spoke in her soft, low voice that usually preceded her losing her temper. Hearing her call the attic *my room* made the blood rush to my cheeks, setting them ablaze.

"That's just how stupid you are! This isn't your room! This is the attic. Your room is downstairs with me!" I yelled and ran down the stairs. I made sure to call her Sophie one more time before I slammed the door.

IX

"What are you complaining about?" Denise asked and handed me a pair of scissors. "You've got your own room now. I'd give my right arm to get out of the room I share with my three little sisters. I wish my house had an attic."

Denise was left-handed, so giving her right arm didn't sound like much of a sacrifice to me. We were in the room I no longer shared with Sophie putting the finishing touches on our art project. We'd come in third place two years in a row at the city-wide junior high school art festival. Our re-creation of the first moon landing was sure to at least move us up to second place this year.

"Denise is right," Carol said. She carefully secured Neil Armstrong to the moon's surface. "With Sophie in the attic, we'll have some privacy."

"Yeah, Nia and her friends won't be able to run us out of the room anymore; and we can listen to the music we want to listen to without her always complaining," Stacy added.

"Don't call her that, Stacy. I mean it," I warned and pointed the scissors at her to make sure she knew I was serious.

"You need to lighten up, Arnetta," Carol said as she handed Denise a pretty good-looking replica of Apollo 11. "We'll come over next weekend and help you fix the room up the way you want it."

"We can pretend we're college students moving into our own apartment," Stacy said. "It'll be fun. Come on, Arnetta. This isn't the end of the world."

"I bet Miss Brenda will even let you paint it purple. It'll be cool. You'll see," Carol said and flashed one of her big toothy grins at me. "We can help you make curtains and everything. All purple."

I sighed and added a few more craters to the moon's surface. Purple was my favorite color. And I'd always wanted a purple room. Being the little sister, I'd always slept in rooms painted the color

Sophie liked. Maybe they were right. Sophie

sleeping in the attic might turn out to be

okay after all.

Just as I was making up my mind to

make the most of the changes in my house,

things went from bad to worse. It seemed

Sophie and her beloved natural were always

smack dab in the middle of it. Just when I

thought I'd seen the worst—Sophie wearing

a long African dress to St. John one

Sunday—something even worse than that

happened: a letter from Sophie's school.
Letters mailed home always meant
something bad. In our house, a bad report
from school was considered a capital
offense; and Brenda Ann Graves was in
charge of doling out the punishment.

"What are they fighting about now?"
Lester asked. He plopped down on the
purple-and-white checkered bean bag chair
in the middle of my room. Gran and I found
it at a garage sale. She gave me the
additional seven cents it cost so that I could
bring home the twenty-five cent purchase. It
had been a ghastly shade of green before
Carol and I raided the remnants of material
in her mother's sewing room. I closed the

door in hopes of drowning out the sound of Sophie and Mama yelling at each other again.

"I think Sophie got into some trouble at school," I answered and didn't look up from my newest *Right On!* magazine. "A letter came in the mail."

"Whoa," Lester said and whistled. "Nia's in deep on this one."

"Mama already called Daddy. They have to meet with Sophie's principal tomorrow," I said repeating what I'd overheard eavesdropping outside Mama's room as she talked to Gran after dinner.

"Arnetta, do you think Mama and Nia will ever stop fighting?" Lester asked.

"As soon as Sophie stops acting so crazy and presses her nappy head. That's all Mama wants her to do," I answered and pulled the centerfold poster of Michael Jackson carefully from the magazine. I took a look around my newly painted purple walls for just the right spot.

Lester got up from the bean bag chair and opened the door. He paused before leaving the room and looked back at me as I hung the poster of Michael Jackson on the back of my closet door. His perfectly shaped natural took up most of the poster. "There must be a lot of yelling at his house," Lester said in departure looking at the poster of Michael.

I stared at the poster of Michael and

wondered, for the first time, what Mama and

Sophie were really fighting about.

X

"I have had enough of Sophie's nonsense, Leon," Brenda whispered through clinched teeth as they waited in the principal's office sitting on hard wooden chairs. "You had better do something to stop it and stop it right now."

"Let's just wait and see what the man has to say, Brenda," Leon said looking at a picture of President Stephen Grover Cleveland that hung in a large wooden frame behind the principal's desk.

"The Man?" Brenda spat out the words. "The Man, as you call him, happens to be the principal of the very best college preparatory high school in this city, Leon. A high school that is third in the state and tenth in the nation in academic achievement. Ninety-eight percent of the students graduating from Cleveland Prep go on to attend some of the best colleges in the country. Do you know how long the waiting list is to get into Cleveland Prep? No, Sophie's going to stop this foolishness right now. Today."

The Man, Principal Aaron Randall, saved Leon from lashing out at Brenda by entering the office. He held a brown folder in his hands in such a way that both Brenda and Leon could read the printed name written in perfect block letters on the tab:

GRAVES, Sophie. Mr. Randall made his apologies for the wait and took his seat behind the large desk. He didn't offer Leon his hand to shake and instead nodded politely in Brenda's direction before opening the folder. He read quietly to himself for a moment before looking at Brenda.

"I am afraid Sophie's behavior at Cleveland Preparatory Technical School has become problematic," Mr. Randall began as his blue eyes bulged.

"Mr. Randall, thank you so much for taking the time to bring this to our attention. I assure you, Sophie will not cause any more trouble at Cleveland Prep," Brenda said. She put on a smile and used the voice she

reserved for white people whom she felt

powerless against.

"Hold on, Brenda," Leon said and

held up his hand. "I'd like to hear what

problem she's causing."

"Leon, you heard Mr. Randall,"

Brenda said while maintaining eye contact

with Mr. Randall. Her too-big smile

apologized for Leon's presence in the room.

"Sophie's behavior at school is unacceptable

and has to stop immediately."

"What's the behavior that's causing

a problem?" Leon asked ignoring Brenda.

Something in the sound of his voice forced

Aaron Randall to look at him for the first time.

"Well, it's similar to problems many of my colleagues are having with some of the Negro students." Mr. Randall's face began to take on the color of an over-ripe tomato. "We find that Sophie's continuous conversations and activities in support of this so-called 'Black Power Movement' are disruptive and divisive. I have to add that I am very disappointed in her behavior. Sophie is one of our brightest Negro students. Many of the teachers overlooked her behavior and attitude, to say nothing of her appearance, for quite some time because of that. It is now out of hand and must come

to a stop.”

"Mr. Randall," Leon said moving to

the edge of his chair. "Maybe I didn't make

myself clear. I'm trying to find out what my

daughter is *doing* that is causing a problem

here at Cleveland Prep."

"Uh, well, uh, Mr. Graves." Mr.

Randall's words stumbled awkwardly from

his mouth as he flipped through Sophie's

folder. "Here. Here is an example of

Sophie's misconduct." He triumphantly

thrust a piece of paper across the desk at

Leon.

"You got rules against club meetings

at this school?" Leon asked after reading the

flyer. Brenda snatched the paper from his hands and gasped.

"Mr. Randall, we do apologize for Sophie's behavior and her involvement in all this," Brenda said. Her face worked hard to match the same shade of red that colored Mr. Randall's. "We will see that this nonsense stops at once. We do thank you for your patience with her. You know teenagers." She faked a laugh that for a moment drained some of the red from Mr. Randall's face.

"Now hold on, Brenda," Leon said. "This man done took me away from my work today, saying my daughter is causing problems at school. He shows me a flyer for a meeting she wants to have with other students to read a book and talk about it. It was my understanding that books were allowed in schools.”

"Mrs. Graves, I assure you, we encourage intellectual discussion and debate at Cleveland Preparatory Technical School, but the hostile nature of the literature and Sophie’s attitude make it totally unacceptable,” Mr. Randall explained and dismissed Leon with a quick glance. His attention once again solely focused on Brenda. “All her talk about ‘Black’ this and ‘Black’ that is troubling to many of our students. Some of the teachers are quite disturbed as well.”

"Mr. Randall, *I* understand. I will talk to Sophie at once," Brenda said and nodded to assure him.

"Well, *I* don't!" Leon said. The sound of his voice an indication his temper was rising. "Seem to me you wasn't troubled a bit last year when them little white girls left Sophie and some of the other Black students out of that fancy art club. And I'd put money on the fact that you didn't call that little white boy's parents in here to talk about how he purposely gave Sophie and some of the other Black students the wrong directions to the program over at that museum either. You didn't seem to care that my daughter and her friends were *troubled* by that. What, Mr. Randall? You only call meetings when your white students get troubled? Is that it?"

"Leon." Brenda squawked, outraged by his words.

"Mr. Graves," Mr. Randall said standing to his feet. "I resent your implication and accusation. Any problem a Cleveland Preparatory Technical School student has is my concern."

"Well, you know what I resent," Leon said, now on his feet. "I resent you wasting my time with this nonsense."

"Mr. Randall, is everything okay in here?" A beefy, large white man with a whistle around his neck opened the door and glared at Leon.

"Yes, Mr. Peters," Mr. Randall answered. He took a few quick breaths and tried to regain his composure. The beefy man with the whistle gave Mr. Randall a look that said he did not believe him.

"I'll be right out here if you need me," Mr. Peters said and took another look at Leon before he closed the door.

"Mr. Randall, I must apologize for Sophie's father's outburst. He has not been involved with Sophie's educational program as closely as I have and does not understand the seriousness of this matter the way we do," Brenda said in her conciliatory voice.

"Please rest assured that Sophie will return to school tomorrow with a change in behavior, attitude, *and* appearance."

"Just so you understand Mrs. Graves, we have Sophie's best interest in mind," Mr. Randall said. He pulled a large handkerchief from his pocket and wiped his forehead.

"The only person in this room even thinking about Sophie is me," Leon said and picked up his hat from the desk. "And unless you plan on showing me a rule against a club that meets to talk about books they read, then you'd do well to stop wasting my time. I can assure you, Mr. Randall that you have yet to see disruptive and divisive behavior."

"I would think discussing Sophie's education and future at Cleveland Preparatory Technical School would be a good use of your time, Mr. Graves," Mr. Randall said coating each word in sarcasm and contempt.

"Is this club keeping my daughter from her regular class work?" Leon asked. The look in his eyes told Mr. Randall that he was finished playing with him.

"Well, no," Mr. Randall stammered. The tomato red color returned to his face.

"Did Sophie tell any of your 'troubled' students that they could not read the book and come to the meeting?" Leon fired the questions like an experienced

litigator.

"Well, no. But…uh," Mr. Randall

said quietly. He now recognized defeat.

"Then you have a good day, Mr.

Randall," Leon said. He turned and left the

office. Brenda made another quick apology

and thanked Mr. Randall for his time and

concern before hurrying to catch up with

Leon.

"How dare you embarrass me like

that in front of Mr. Randall?" Brenda

snapped through clinched teeth when she

reached the parking lot. Leon climbed into

the cab of his pickup truck and started the

engine.

"You embarrassed yourself, Brenda. You were in there grinning, bowing, and scraping in front of that peckerwood. Have you even talked to our daughter about what's going on up here? Did you even try to get her side of this? Did you know some of the white teachers are trying to get the Board of Education to ban her and the other Black students from wearing afros? You shoulda been in there defending our daughter instead of kissing Randall's ass," Leon fired back. He felt the muscles in his jaws tighten. His anger was in full effect. "And don't you ever apologize to a white man for me. Ever."

"You have no right to talk to me like this, Leon. You see Sophie twice a month. You don't know what I've been going through with her these last few months. I'm trying to make sure she has a chance in this world. Something you obviously don't care about since you walked out on her," Brenda spat out with her eyes blazing.

Leon put the truck in gear. "Let me try and make this clear to you. I walked out on *you*, Brenda. You. Not Sophie. The sad thing is, you probably don't even know why."

Brenda moved away from the truck as though Leon had struck her. Tears stung her eyes and held on to her lashes as she

walked back to her car.

Leon rolled down the windows and

welcomed the bite of the cool autumn

morning. It was at times like this that he had

trouble remembering he had been in love

with Brenda since he was fourteen years old.

He had met Brenda the summer before ninth

grade. His grandmother had forced him and

his younger sister Lula to go to a Sunday

school convention in Birmingham, Alabama.

Leon remembered the day….

He almost wished he had decided to go pick cotton with Eddie as he rode in the back of his Uncle Otis' pickup truck. He hated every minute of the almost two-hour ride between Birmingham and his hometown of Mountain Brook, Alabama. He spent his time blocking out his sister's non-stop chattering by devising a plan to ditch the Sunday school convention and see some of the big city. He had just thought up a fool-proof escape plan and a way to buy his sister's silence, when Uncle Otis' pickup truck pulled up behind several cars in front of Allen Chapel AME Church.

"Leon! Leon!" Otis called. "Boy, grab your bag and get out this truck." Otis followed his nephew's gaze over to the pretty, smiling face of one of the youth greeters. Otis let out a huge laugh. "Look like this Sunday school convention ain't gone be so hard on you after all. Huh, Nephew?"

"What you talking about, Uncle Otis?" Leon asked. He smoothed down his shirt and hopped out the truck bed. "I love Sunday school conventions."

"Yeah, right," Otis said and shook his head. "You keep up with Lula and don't let that pretty little thing get your behind in no trouble. Your grandmother sent you here

to get right with Jesus." Otis laughed again.

His nephew's interest in the pretty girl

brought back fond memories of a few

Sunday school conventions from his youth.

"Uncle Otis, tell Grandma you left

me standing among angels," Leon said. He

slapped his uncle on the back and headed

toward the welcoming committee table.

As Leon's memory receded, he said

aloud, "I wonder where the girl I met all

those years ago went." He scratched his

head and continued to drive down the street.

XI

"What did Miss Brenda say?" Janet asked as she stitched a large, black piece of fabric to an equally large red piece of fabric.

"You know my mama," Nia said. She rolled her eyes and worked on the stitches between the black piece of fabric and a green piece of fabric. "The same old stuff about me being rebellious and what kind of future will I have if I don't graduate from Cleveland Prep and more threats about pressing my hair. It's like she doesn't even see what's going on.

"We all remember what happened to Nicole Anderson almost five months ago.

We were studying for our biology mid-term at Tanya's house when her father called us to the den.

"The news reported a fifteen-year-old girl had been killed by a police officer during a demonstration. We all stared at the TV in disbelief as Nicole's photo flashed on the screen. I got pissed off when the police spokeperson described Nicole's murder as a case of self-defense. Why did that pig need to fire ten shots to defend himself against somebody who is unarmed?

"At that moment, I knew I could no longer stand on the sidelines. It's time we FIGHT for justice and equality. Sophie wouldn't join the fight, but Nia would."

All of the girls had tears in their eyes after Nia finished. "That's a day we'll never forget," Deborah somberly said. "Nia, I know you and your mother aren't getting along right now, but how'd you get her to let you come over here?" asked Janet who was now cutting black fabric in the shape of the African continent.

"I didn't. I told her I was going to the library to study for my French exam," Nia said as Tanya burst into the room carrrying a large, brown paper bag.

"Where have you been, Tanya?" Deborah asked.

"What's that smell?" Janet asked.
Her nose crinkled as she waved her hand in front of her face.

"Tanya, are you high? And who let you in the house?" Nia asked. She rushed to close Janet's bedroom door before one of Janet's parents came up to her room.

"Yeah. And hungry as a horse with a capital 'H'. Janet's little brother let me in. Dang, y'all paranoid." Tanya laughed. She looked around and noticed the gloomy look on her friends' faces. "Why do y'all look like somebody just died?" Tanya asked while taking a package of Hostess Cupcakes from the bag and flopping down on Janet's bed.

"Nia reminded us of Nicole Anderson and why we're doing this. Anyway, you better get that weed smell out of your hair before you get home," Deborah said. She pulled a Nehi Orange soda from the bag. "If your mama smells that, you won't live to see the revolution."

"You must've been with Roderick," Nia said. She stopped her work on the African liberation flag. She took the package of Hostess Twinkies from Janet. "He stays high."

"Don't start in on Rod, Nia," Tanya warned already starting on her second package of cupcakes. "He fine and got a car.

And his mama works nights." She laughed too loudly.

"You are so nasty." Deborah laughed even though she tried to keep a straight face. "Did you forget we had this flag to work on, Sister?"

"Yeah. Sorry." Tanya licked chocolate frosting from her fingers. "It looks good though."

"You know we got to have this ready for the renaming ceremony at the community center on Friday night. Don't start flaking out on us now, Tanya," Janet said. She returned to working on the flag.

"I can finish it up on my machine," Nia said. She made a few more stitches to

tack the strips in place. "Tanya, you know
you're out of line showing up late and
messed up. This is for Nicole and the others
we've lost in the struggle."

Attempting to change the subject,
Tanya said, "I saw Jamal at the gas station.
He asked about you, Nia."

"What did he say?" Nia asked. She
focused on folding the flag and tried not to
look too pleased.

"Oh, don't even try to look like you
don't care." Janet laughed and tossed a
potato chip at Nia, which lightened the
mood in the room. "You know you're crazy
about that boy."

"He *is* fine," Deborah said and slapped Tanya five.

"He just said to say hi," Tanya said. She drank a carton of chocolate milk in a few gulps, then reached for a bag of Cheetos.

"I haven't been able to talk to or see him in almost a week." Nia sighed as only teenage girls are able. "My mama's watching me like a hawk."

"Well, go to your dad's this weekend. I'm sure you'll get to see him then. And he'll be at the community center Friday night," Janet said. "You kiss him yet?"

"Kiss him?" Tanya said while looking at her friends. "I hope you doing more than that with that fine brotha."

"Ain't nobody trying to get pregnant, Tanya," Deborah said and looked at Nia for confirmation.

"What?" Tanya asked. "Me and Rod are careful."

"So was Aileen Martin. Now she's *visiting* her aunt Lorraine in Little Rock, Arkansas," Janet said. "How much you want to bet that visit ends in about seven months."

"You think she'll come back to Cleveland Prep?" Deborah asked as she and Nia carefully finished folding the flag.

"I wouldn't," Janet answered and threw a French book at Tanya. "Everybody knows what happened with her and Alonzo."

"Well, ain't nothing happening with me and Jamal like that," Nia said shaking her head. "All of us have a deal anyway, right? College first."

"Right," Janet, Deborah, and Tanya answered in unison. The friends laughed and settled down to their studies.

I heard the front door open and wished Lester had been quicker getting his coat. I was hoping we'd already be gone before Sophie came home. I rushed into the hallway and hoped she would see me and rush up the stairs to her attic room before Mama got to the hallway.

"Nia, we going for ice cream!" Lester announced running into the hallway.

"Sophie is not going with us for ice cream," Mama said. She held her keys in her hand and glared at Sophie.

"Hello, Mama," Sophie said in that voice she used to let you know she was not stooping to your level. Mama put on her jacket and didn't respond.

"Bring me back a scoop of cherry vanilla," Gran called out from the kitchen. "And Arnetta make sure Perry scoop from the end with lots of cherries."

"Okay, Gran," I answered back.

"Come on before Mr. Perry closes," Lester pleaded and reached for Mama's hand.

The way Mama and Sophie were looking at each other, we might not make it to Mr. Perry's if they got a chance to go at it. I wish there was a way I could warn Sophie to go to her room and fast. Mama had been in a foul mood all evening until Gran suggested ice cream. It looked as if she was forgetting the troubles of her day until

she saw Sophie and that natural.

"Nia, why can't you come with us?"

Lester asked as Mama opened the front

door.

"I wasn't invited, Lester," Sophie

said simply and headed toward the stairs.

Mama mumbled something about not taking

her nappy head anywhere and walked out

the front door. I followed wondering if

Sophie even remembered how much she

loved Mr. Perry's banana splits.

XII

"Hey there, 'Little Sister'. You come

to help in the liberation of our people?"

Jamal asked looking over his shoulder as his

arm turned the handle of the mimeograph

machine. He winked at Sophie.

I adjusted my eyes to the shadows in

Uncle Eddie's garage and looked around.

Sophie and Janet were busy painting signs

while Deborah and Tanya hammered

already painted signs onto sticks. There

were three or four boys, all wearing those

African shirts, working in the garage. I

recognized the smell of the incense Sophie

burned in her room and heard the rhythmic

drum beat of African music. I covered my ears.

"Uncle Eddie know you out here messing around in his garage? You know he has valuable equipment out here," I said and hoped the look on my face captured the look of disgust Mama used to make people feel stupid.

"Arnetta. Help or go away," Sophie said in a voice that said she was trying to be patient with me. "We have lots of work to do and no time to fool with you."

"Let her stay, Nia. She's okay," Jamal said. His words worked better than my glaring because Sophie gave him a quick smile and went back to her work.

I heard footsteps behind me and turned to see Aunt Ruthie carrying a large, covered tray.

"Three cheers for Aunt Ruthie," Deborah said and paused from the work to clap. One of the Dashikis rushed to help Aunt Ruthie with the tray of sandwiches. June followed. He was pulling a cooler and wearing a dashiki. I made a gagging noise when he passed me. I did the best eye rolling I could muster when he looked my way.

"Righteous," another Dashiki exclaimed. He reached into the cooler and pulled a bottle of grape soda from among the ice. He slapped June five and took a bite out of the sandwich that Janet handed him from the tray.

"My small but delicious contribution to the revolution." Aunt Ruthie laughed.

"Power to the people," Tanya said. She raised her right fist in the Black Power salute as her left hand guided a big ham sandwich to her mouth.

"And, Aunt Ruthie," Sophie said. She kissed Aunt Ruthie on the cheek.

"There's banana pudding in the refrigerator when you're ready. Clean up after yourselves," Aunt Ruthie instructed. "I'm taking the kids to the movies. Nia, your daddy and uncle will be back around seven.

Make sure this garage looks like a garage again before then."

"It'll look like we were never here," Jamal said. "Thanks again Mrs. Graves for letting us use the garage today."

"Mama, can I stay and help? Please," June pleaded as Aunt Ruthie turned to leave.

I set a frown hard and deep on my face waiting for Aunt Ruthie to tell June to take his behind to the car.

"If it's all right with Nia and her friends, June. It's okay with me," Aunt Ruthie said. She looked first at June's pleading face and then at Sophie who nodded. I felt nauseous.

"Right On!" June squeaked in his changing boy-man voice.

"Come on, Little Brother. I'll show you how to work the mimeograph machine while I finish my speech for the rally. We need plenty of flyers. Maybe tomorrow after church you can help us pass them out in the neighborhood." Jamal placed his arm around June's shoulders as they walked toward the machine.

I groaned loudly and stomped out of the garage behind Aunt Ruthie. I also made sure to get in one last eye roll at Sophie and that natural of hers.

I loved everything about the movies,

and going to the movies with Aunt Ruthie

and my cousins only added to the fun.

Before Sophie got too grown-up and stopped

being my sister and Daddy moved out of the

house, she would take me and Lester to a

matinee on Saturday after we finished our

chores around the house. Daddy would drop

us off and go spend a few hours with Uncle

Eddie. Mama always gave us money for our

favorite snacks—popcorn with lots of butter

for me, Milk Duds for Lester, and Red Vines

for Sophie—along with instructions on how to behave out of her sight....

*"Sophie, you make sure Lester goes to the bathroom **before** you go into the theater."*

"Arnetta, remember to get lots of napkins so you can wipe all that butter off your fingers."

"Sophie, stay away from that Turner boy. I hear he cleans up at the theater. He's too old for you."

"Yes, Mama," we would respond in unison as we moved toward the front door. Once Daddy started the car, all rules were forgotten.

Now, Lester and I went to the drive-in with Aunt Ruthie and our cousins once a month. Aunt Ruthie said it was too many of us to keep up with at a movie theater. Joseph would always get to fussing, and we would have to leave before the end of the movie. I missed going to the theater with Sophie, but there was something fun about the drive-in too.

On the way back home that night, things didn't seem so bad after all. At least not until Rachel opened her big mouth.

"Mama, you think the police gone put Nia and her friends in jail like they did those teenagers on the news the other

night?"

I turned to look at Aunt Ruthie and

caught the 'shut up' look she gave Rachel

over my head. "I'm sure Nia and her friends

will be fine, Rachel."

"Fine doing what?" I asked. "Why

would the police bother Sophie? Aunt

Ruthie what is Rachel talking about?"

"Rachel is talking about something

she doesn't know enough about," Aunt

Ruthie said sternly. "Don't worry about Nia.

She's a smart girl."

"Her name is not Nia. It is Sophie.

Sophie Leona Graves. And she hasn't been

acting so smart lately, in case you haven't

noticed." I braced myself for the likely smack in the mouth I would probably get in the next five seconds for backtalking Aunt Ruthie. Instead she just gave me a look that told me I had gotten away with one, but I wouldn't be so lucky if it happened again. She didn't have to worry about that. "Mama says Sophie's acting like she doesn't have the sense she was born with."

"What do *you* say, Arnetta?" Aunt Ruthie asked. The tone of her voice let me know she was really interested. Aunt Ruthie was one of those rare grown-ups who really listened to what kids had to say. "I already know what Brenda thinks. I'd like to know what you think about what your sister and her friends are doing." Aunt Ruthie pulled into the driveway.

I stared straight ahead at the quiet and dark garage. I saw Jamal's truck still parked at the curb and figured they were all inside eating up all the banana pudding, listening to records, and dancing. I didn't answer Aunt Ruthie's question. Not because I was angry or trying to be stubborn. I didn't answer the question because I didn't have an answer. I didn't know what I thought about any of it. I'd been so busy listening to Mama and Sophie fight about what *they* thought that I hadn't taken the time to think anything for myself.

"I don't know," I answered softly and dropped my head.

"Make up your own mind on this thing, Arnetta," Aunt Ruthie said as the car doors opened and my cousins piled out. "What *Nia* and her friends are doing along with other kids across this country is going to change your life. You can't stand on what your mama thinks. Now go inside and take your bath. We got church in the morning. And, Arnetta?"

"Yes, Aunt Ruthie," I answered. I was already thinking about how I would answer her question.

"Don't get your hair wet." Aunt Ruthie smiled as she got out of the car. The twinkle in her eyes told me, whether it felt

like it or not, everything would be all right.

XIII

Nia was careful to close the door to Jamal's pickup truck quietly even though she was almost two blocks from the house. She walked slowly toward her house and was glad she would have some time alone there. It would give her a chance to think. She remembered not to drop her book bag on the chair in the hallway and decided to go to the kitchen for a quick snack before she went up to her room.

She stopped suddenly upon entering the kitchen, which caused her large silver hoop earrings to gently brush against her cheeks because of the abrupt stop.

Gran was seated at the kitchen table holding a folded paperback novel in her large, brown hands.

"Gran, you feeling all right?" Nia asked. She quickly placed a casual look on her face and hoped Gran did not see the panic in her eyes. "You're home early."

"I was just about to say the same thing to you," Gran said in her soothing voice. A serious look made its way across her face. Her voice alone moved Nia to sit on one of the kitchen chairs.

"I got suspended," Nia answered the question Gran's eyes asked.

"I figured that part out when Mr. Randall's secretary called to remind your mama to be sure to sign your suspension

form tonight so that the teachers could give

you the work you missed the last three days.

I want to know why."

"The racist administration at

Cleveland Prep…," Nia began. She sat up

straighter in her chair for emphasis almost in

defiance.

"Girl, don't give me no speech,"

Gran said with eyes narrowed in warning.

Nia swallowed hard. "I want to know how a

girl bright as you got herself kicked out of

one of the finest schools in the city."

"Some of us were passing out flyers

for the big rally at the community center at

school. It was during lunch, so we didn't

think it would be a problem. Somebody gave Mr. Randall a flyer. He called us into his office and told us we couldn't pass out what he called 'riotous literature' on school grounds." Nia paused. She checked Gran's face and saw the irritation evaporating and continued. "So we started passing them out after school, across the street at McDonald's. Mr. Randall came over and told us to stop. We told him, NO."

Gran took off her reading glasses and squeezed the bridge of her nose.

"Gran, I didn't do anything wrong. Mr. Randall is asking for public apologies from all of us for 'embarrassing the good students of Cleveland Preparatory Technical

School' and some mess about disrupting the harmony of the school. The suspension is over tomorrow. I've been going to the library every day. Today, I went to the community center to help Jamal set up the chairs and hang the flag we made for the meeting on Saturday. There's going to be an assembly tomorrow for us to apologize in front of the entire student body." Nia stopped speaking and took a deep breath before she continued. "I am not apologizing." The resolve in her voice was unmistakable.

"What's gone happen to you if you don't apologize?" Gran asked and tried not to hold her breath.

"I don't know. Mr. Randall didn't say. I think he just expects us to give in," Nia said. "But I will not apologize for my participation in the rally, passing out flyers, or my commitment to the struggle for the liberation of Black people."

"Baby, are you sure about all this? Cause you sticking your neck way out on this one." Gran asked.

Nia nodded. "Gran, you remember when you told me about how you *had* to leave Grandpa? About how you knew it would be hard because Mama and Aunt Teresa were just babies, but you knew you had to leave or something inside of you would die?" Nia's eyes sparkled with unshed tears. "That's how this feels for me, Gran. I don't know how it's going to all work out. I just know that if I back down, a part of me will die."

"You go on upstairs," Gran said. "I'll talk to your mama, Nia."

XIV

I was glad for the movie, about the migration of whales, Mr. Dennis had decided to show in biology. I had been having a hard time concentrating since my talk with Aunt Ruthie last weekend. I knew I had to get it together before next period. I had an oral report to make on the fall of the Roman Empire and my straight-A report card was at stake, but I couldn't get Aunt Ruthie's words out of my head....

"Arnetta, you got to find a way to stop being so mad at your sister," Aunt Ruthie said. Her hands were rapidly shelling

the peas we would have for dinner on Sunday. They dropped into the bowl poised between her knees so fast they sounded like a machine gun being fired. "You need to take time to understand a thing before you decide to hate it."

"Mama says Sophie just acting a fool," I said and clumsily opened the shell of some peas. My pea shelling skills were nowhere near that of Aunt Ruthie's.

"That's what I'm talking about," Aunt Ruthie said. "You're angry with Nia because your mother is angry with her. That's no good, Arnetta. You're not a little girl anymore. It's time you find out what you need to know to make up your own mind.

Then, if YOU think Nia is being foolish, so be it." Aunt Ruthie handed me another fistful of peas. "Just remember, 'cause it's foolish to you, don't make it so."

Make up your own mind. I wasn't even sure what I needed to know to make up my mind. I hadn't thought much about the world before Sophie's natural moved into our house. My 'world' consisted of Washington Junior High School, home, Uncle Eddie and Aunt Ruthie's, and St. John AME Church. I liked it like that and was just trying to keep Sophie's 'world' of demonstrations, rallies, and nappy heads away from mine. Each day that was getting

harder and harder to do. I needed some help.

"I'll meet you guys at the library. I

left my notebook in Mr. Lindsey's room," I

lied and backed away from Stacy, Denise,

and Carol as they walked toward the stairs

leading to the school's second floor library. I

turned away before they could offer to wait

and ran down the hall toward Mr. Lindsey's

room. *Make up your own mind.* I heard Aunt

Ruthie's words again as I knocked on the

door.

"Come on in," Mr. Lindsey called

out. "Hi, Arnetta." He stood at the

blackboard writing the next day's algebra

assignment in his perfect penmanship. His

fingertips held the long piece of chalk like a painter held a brush. At the beginning of the school year, I (just like every other seventh-grade girl in his homeroom) had a big crush on Mr. Lindsey. While I still felt like giggling for no reason sometimes when he passed me in the hall and said good morning, the crush ended when Gran and I saw him and *Mrs.* Lindsey at Woolworth's one Saturday morning.

"Mr. Lindsey, what do you think about the Black Power Movement? My sister, Sophie, is *really* into it. She even wants to be called 'Nia' and wears a natural and everything. She stopped going to St. John and now goes every Sunday to St.

Luke because they don't talk about her hair or her African dresses over there. She and that natural are driving my mama crazy. They yell at each other all the time; and when we go for ice cream, Mama won't let Sophie go with us or bring her a banana split. And, Mama knows banana splits are Sophie's favorite." Tears flooded my eyes as the words came pouring out as if something had exploded inside me. "I'm tired of being mad at Sophie, and I'm tired of my mama yelling." I burst into tears and covered my face with both hands. I didn't think about being embarrassed until Mr. Lindsey handed me a clean, white handkerchief. He waited while I wiped my face and blew my nose.

"Sit down, Arnetta," Mr. Lindsey said. He pointed to the desk where Stacy usually sat and then he sat at Carol's desk. "I'm sorry you have been so upset. It must all seem pretty scary to you right now. You asked me what I think about the Black Power Movement. I think our country is a place where people can change things when they aren't happy with things as they currently are. Change can be frightening. I think some really good things will come from this; and that our people, Black people, need something good to happen for us. I am afraid that some very bad things are likely to happen too."

"Mr. Lindsey, why do you think my mama is so mad at Sophie? They used to laugh together all the time. Mama used to even take Sophie and her friends shopping, out to dinner, and to do fun stuff. Now, my mama acts like she hates Sophie." I started to cry again and wondered if I'd ever stop. I blew my nose on Mr. Lindsey's handkerchief again.

"I think your mother is like some of the rest of us, Arnetta. Afraid. Things are changing quickly in the world around her, and she does not know what to do. It is probably even scarier for your mother because some of that change has ended up in her home." Mr. Lindsey paused and waited for my latest crying spell to pass. "Some of us are not used to Black people talking like these kids do and demanding rights instead of politely asking for them."

"Things aren't going to go back to how they were before all this. Are they, Mr. Lindsey?" I asked, only sniffling now.

"No they will not, Arnetta," he said looking directly at me. "I am not sure they should."

"Thank you, Mr. Lindsey," I said. All my tears seemed to be gone now. Talking to Mr. Lindsey had been a good idea. I'd wash and press his handkerchief before I did my homework tonight and return it to him tomorrow.

"You are welcome," Mr. Lindsey said standing. "Arnetta." I stopped at the door and turned back to face him. "Take small bites out of change. Don't try to swallow it all at once," he stated and then returned to his work at the blackboard.

<h1 style="text-align:center">XV</h1>

Nia walked into the newly painted auditorium and took her seat along with the rest of her homeroom class. A chill that began at the base of her spine and ran up her neck caused her to shiver despite the heater being on full blast. Vice Principal Benson avoided looking at her when he took the podium. He asked students to get seated and 'still themselves'. This was his patrician way of saying be quiet. Nia tried to take deep breaths, like those she had learned in the yoga classes she took at the community center, to calm her nerves. Mr. Benson's voice droned on and on about the 'special privilege of attending Cleveland Preparatory

Technical School' and the importance of

'preserving a tranquil learning

environment'. She hoped he would speak

long enough to give her yoga breathing time

to slow her heartbeat and bring it back to its

normal rhythm. Mr. Benson made a plea for

volunteers to clean up after an upcoming

school activity and then stepped aside. Mr.

Randall walked slowly to the podium. After

adjusting the microphone stand to

accommodate his taller height, he cleared

his throat and focused his gaze on Nia. She

met his gaze and then did what her

grandmother always told her to do when she

found herself between a rock and a hard place—pray.

Nia took another deep breath as 250 pairs of eyes looked at her. Mr. Randall called her name for the third time.

"Sophie Graves, come now and apologize to the Cleveland Preparatory Technical School's community of learners and educators for contaminating their learning environment with vile and divisive attitudes and behaviors." Mr. Randall's right foot tapped his impatience on the hardwood floor of the auditorium's stage.

Nia remained still in her seat. She thought she might be losing her mind when she recognized the sound of clapping coming from her left. She glanced quickly and saw several Black students clapping. When Cleveland Prep's track star Lamont Jackson stood and raised his left fist in the familiar Black Power salute, the rest of the Black students joined him. Mr. Randall yelled into the microphone demanding quiet. He pounded the podium with his fist as Myra Buchannan and Betty Forester, Cleveland Prep's very blond and blue-eyed junior class president and vice president, jumped to their feet clapping. Mr. Randall called for teachers to clear the auditorium just as Mr. Benson tapped her on the shoulder and commanded in a voice that rang out over the noise in the auditorium,

"To the office, Miss Graves."

Nia exited the auditorium to cheers

of 'Right On, Sister!' She followed Mr.

Benson down the hall toward the office. She

could hear students singing what she

considered the Black Power anthem (James

Brown's "Say It Loud I'm Black and I'm

Proud") coming from the auditorium. The

sound of Miss Clark's Selectric typewriter

met Nia's ears as she entered the office.

"Ticky-Ticky-Ticky. Bing." Nia knew

without looking that all that typing had

something to do with her. Miss Clark paused

her typing long enough to give her a look

that displayed her complete disapproval in

her olive green eyes. Miss Clark finished her typing, then carefully removed the document from the typewriter and rushed into Mr. Randall's office.

"Mr. Randall will see you now," Miss Clark said. She held the door open for Nia to enter the room. Miss Clark shook her head slowly, muttered something under her breath, and closed the door behind her.

"This is a very regrettable day, Miss Graves," Mr. Randall spoke in what the students called his 'undertaker voice' behind his back. "Cleveland Preparatory Technical School has gone over and beyond the call of duty to bring *you students* into our elite learning family."

Nia made sure not to roll her eyes. Mr. Randall's emphasis on the words *you students* made his feelings clear.

"I'll give you one last chance to apologize and vow to keep your misguided opinions to yourself and out of Cleveland Preparatory Technical School. That *hair* will also have to go." He paused and gave the look that usually brought students to tears. "I will not wait all day for your answer."

Nia took a look at the pen Mr. Randall held in his hand. The word EXPULSION jumped off the page and seemed to dance before her eyes in neon. She took another yoga-deep breath and looked him straight in the eyes.

"Thank you, Mr. Randall. But, I don't need another chance," Nia stated. "I will not apologize for working for the cause of obtaining equal rights and justice for Black people. Ever."

"Very well then," Mr. Randall choked out through pencil-thin lips. He cleared his throat and signed his name in several places on the document and called for Miss Clark. "Please have Sophie's locker cleaned out immediately."

"It has already been done, Mr. Randall." Miss Clark shoved a box into Nia's arms with a look of satisfaction plastered across her crow-like face.

"You are to leave this campus immediately," Mr. Randall said. He stood and handed Nia a copy of the expulsion document. "Miss Clark, be sure to notify Mrs. Graves."

"Yes, Mr. Randall." Miss Clark held the door for Nia to leave the office.

"This won't stop us, you know," Nia said over her shoulder as she left the office.

XVI

I came home on a Wednesday afternoon and found Daddy's pickup truck in front of the house. Daddy's pickup truck was only in front of our house on the Saturday mornings he picked up Lester for their trip to the barbershop. As if this were not shocking enough, Tanya and Jamal were carrying large boxes out the front door.

"Tanya, what are you doing?" I asked while running up the front steps.

"Go inside, Arnetta." Tanya glanced at me quickly and then looked away.

I didn't want Jamal calling me 'Little Sister', so I decided not to say anything to him and ran through the open front door.

"Gran! Mama! What's going on?" I yelled dropping my books in a heap in the hallway and rushed to the kitchen. "Gran! Mama!"

"Arnetta, stop all that noise," Gran said and waved me into the kitchen.

I wasn't the only one in the house yelling. I could hear my mother's voice muffled by her closed bedroom door; but her voice was still loud, too loud. And was that Daddy yelling back? This was bad. I had to get in there. Gran grabbed my arm as I turned to leave the kitchen.

"Gran, what's going on? Why's Daddy here? Why are they yelling at each other? What's the matter?" I asked these series of questions in rapid fire. Not knowing what was going on frightened me.

"Your sister got expelled from Cleveland Prep today," Gran answered. "Her and your mama had a big fight, and Nia called your daddy. She's moving to his place."

Moving to his place? I felt like I'd been punched in the stomach. Sophie was leaving? This wasn't just a trip up the stairs to her attic room. She wouldn't even be in the house. I heard Mama yelling clearly now as she and Daddy came toward the kitchen. I had to put a stop to this. Was everybody in my family crazy?

"Daddy, don't take Sophie away!" I yelled rushing into his arms. He smelled of sweat, motor oil, and brake fluid. I buried my face in his coveralls.

"Arnetta, get out of the way; and stop all your foolishness," Mama yelled. She tried to loosen the vice grip I had around Daddy's waist. If I could just hold him here, he couldn't take Sophie away.

"Come on, Nettie-girl. You getting yourself all upset for nothing," Daddy said and held me close. "Nia's gonna be right at the house with me and Lester when you get there on Saturday."

"I want her to stay here, Daddy," I said. Tears streamed down my face. My heart broke into pieces with each tear.

"Arnetta, you gone have to be my big girl on this one," Daddy said. He bent down and removed the tears from my cheeks with his hands. "Nia need to do this right now. We got to help her. Okay?"

I wiped my nose on the back of my hand, not caring that Mama was watching, and tried to find Daddy's 'big girl' somewhere in the pain I was feeling. I offered him a weak smile. It was the best I had at the moment.

"That's my big girl," Daddy said and hugged me for my effort. "Now run over to

Mrs. Watkins' place and bring your brother home so he can see Nia before we leave."

I glanced at Mama and headed to the front door. Her face had turned into a stone mask.

I ran into Sophie going up the front steps as I was running down.

"Hey Arnetta, will you hold on to something for me?" she asked. She pulled the small, black wooden fist that hung around her neck on a felt string over her head. She had made it in a woodshop class she'd taken at the community center a few months ago. I hadn't seen her take it off since. I stepped forward so she could place it over my head. "Sure," I said staring at my sister in awe. I couldn't believe she would trust me with something that was so special to her. "Thanks, Nia."

"You're welcome, Little Sister." Nia smiled her first smile at me in months.

I smiled back.

XVII

The world didn't stop changing. It seemed to change faster every day, but I got used to it. Stacy's brother Clayton got drafted into the army and went to Vietnam. Mr. Lindsey helped me find Vietnam on a map, and my homeroom class wrote Clayton letters every week so he wouldn't feel so alone. I started calling my sister 'Nia' and didn't mind it anymore when Jamal called me 'Little Sister'. Nia organized the first Black Student Union at her new school: Monroe High School. She even got arrested at an anti-war demonstration at city hall. Aunt Ruthie started wearing a natural, and

June insisted on being called Abdul. I slipped every once in a while and called him June, but I always corrected myself. He hung posters of Huey Newton and Angela Davis on his wall and declared himself a Black Panther. Mama started to smile again; and the last time we went for ice cream, we stopped by Daddy's so Nia could join us. She and Mama even shared a banana split. Lester finally taught Lucky how to fetch a ball.

I still went with Mama to *Rena's House of Beauty* the first and third Saturday of each month to get my hair pressed and curled. However, I was making up my own mind about everything else that was going

on in the world. I never changed my name
nor wore African dresses, but one Saturday I
found myself in Uncle Eddie's garage
making signs that read **POWER TO THE
PEOPLE**. And, I was glad.

Epilogue

I sifted through the box of CDs I kept in the bottom drawer of the file cabinet near the window. "Here you are," I said aloud. My voice seemed to echo throughout the quiet, empty classroom. I pressed the POWER button on the CD player, pushed the top so it would spring open, and inserted the CD Nia had sent me last month for my birthday. I smiled at the words on the label she had created for the CD she had burned. It contained many of the songs that had filled my childhood and teenage years. Nia had written, in her calligraphy-like script, the words *For The Struggle* across the metallic silver disk. I pressed the PLAY button and waited.

Aretha Franklin's soulful voice encouraged me to keep my 'rock steady'. The music seemed right for the stillness of my classroom at the end of the day. As Stevie Wonder was telling me about the struggles of 'living for the city', I heard a knock on the door. I glanced at the clock and wondered who was still in the building at 4:35 p.m. on a Friday. The halls had cleared quickly over an hour ago. Students had rushed to buses or cars to take them across town for tonight's football game, and teachers had rushed to get anywhere that would allow them to forget about tests, book reports, and teenagers.

"Come in," I called. I turned the music down so whoever was on the other side of the door could hear me.

"Ms. Graves, you got a minute?" Che'reese Miller stuck her head through the small opening she made with the door.

"Yes, Che'reese. I *have* a minute," I answered. I sounded more like my mother than I would ever admit. I waved her in and walked toward the door. She glanced quickly over her shoulder and opened the door wider. Darius, Michael, Talisha, and Angelo moved past her and into the room. "Well, hello."

"Ms. Graves. We want to ask you something," Talisha announced. That seemed to be their cue. They all took seats. I joined them by sitting at the desk nearest Che'reese and waited to see what had brought five high school juniors to my classroom on a Friday long after school had ended. I knew for sure that at least four of them (Michael did not hang out) usually would be found rooting for the Cleveland Wildcats on a Friday evening during football season.

"We can't stop thinking about what you told us today in class," Darius said. "About your sister and her friends."

"Yeah. And about your family and how everybody didn't start out on the same page," Angelo added. Che'reese patted him on the shoulder. He had confided in me a couple months ago that his parents had separated. From the looks on the faces of the others, he had told them too.

"What we really want to know is why you became a teacher." Michael's voice again stilled the room. It even seemed to bring a halt to Gladys Knight & The Pips' "Friendship Train " playing on the CD player.

All eyes were on me. Che'reese's sapphire nose ring twinkled as if to encourage me. I momentarily flashed back to the day I'd gone to Mr. Lindsey's room after school to ask a question. My students were doing the same: seeking answers to questions about what was happening in the world around them.

"I guess it's my way of fighting," I said. The words became truer as I spoke them. "My sister Nia and I are different. Nia is all about protest, direct action, and moving forward. I have more of a tendency to hold on, look back."

"Maybe that's why you're such a good history teacher," Talisha blurted with her hands waving in motion. "I wonder…"

"Talisha. Not now," Angelo said as the others glared at her.

"Sorry," she said and quickly put her hands under her lap. The students always teased her by saying the only way to shut her up was to stop her hands from moving.

"Talisha may be on to something," I said and winked at her. "My dad was big on history. He said it was impossible to move forward in any meaningful way without knowing who or what came before you."

"My granny always says, you gotta know where you been before you can go where you going," Darius offered doing his best old-lady imitation.

"History seemed as large a part of the struggle as picket signs and protests," I said. I took in their faces that were so open to receive what I was saying. "The textbooks were never enough."

"So you bought your own." Talisha pointed to the bookcases lining the back walls of my classroom. Some of my colleagues called them 'The Black Stacks'. Many often asked to borrow books to augment their own lesson plans.

"Talisha," the others voiced their need for her to be quiet in unison.

"It's okay." I laughed. "Talisha is right. You must always look for what isn't in the books or movies that others give you. You have to make up your own minds." The words of Aunt Ruthie, from all those years ago, danced around in my head.

"So to *synthesize* what you're saying, Ms. Graves," Angelo stated as we all laughed at the use of the word I often used when asking them to bring their point into focus. "You used history to understand your sister's way of fighting, and now you use it to equip folks to continue the fight for liberation."

"Well said." I smiled. Our applause moved Angelo to take a bow. Naturally.

"Ms. Graves, you know what your daddy and Darius' granny said about history helping people deal with what's going on today makes sense. It's like the Sankofa," Che'reese said. She reached into her backpack and brought out a notebook

covered in vibrant Kente cloth.

"The san what?" Talisha asked.

Che'reese pushed her notebook toward her.

"San. Ko. Fa." Che'reese

pronounced each syllable deliberately. "It

means to go back and get. Its symbol looks

like a bird looking over its shoulder."

I glanced at the notebook and saw

the Andinkra symbols I'd come to know

because of Nia.

"That's it!" Talisha bounced up from

her seat with the notebook in hand. She

wrote the word Sankofa across the

whiteboard in bright red block letters.

"We'll form the Sankofa Club at Cleveland

Prep. We'll study and learn history that's not in the textbooks. We'll encourage other high schools to start chapters, and we'll have a global network of Sankofa Clubs."

"Hold on there, Ms. Black History." Che'reese raised her hand and laughed.

"No. Talisha's got something," Michael said.

"Yeah. I think she does too," Angelo responded in agreement.

"This is our first meeting. That bird will be the logo," Talisha said and tossed the notebook back to Che'reese. "Write that down, Che'reese."

"We'll need a faculty advisor to have the club officially recognized," Darius said.

Five sets of eyes turned to face me.

"Ms. Graves you gotta…," Talisha began "You *have* to be our advisor. Please." Her please started a chorus of pleases and even brought Angelo to the side of my seat on his knees.

"All right. All right." I laughed. The first members of the newly formed Sankofa Club burst into cheers. James Brown even approved as "Say It Loud I'm Black and I'm Proud" made its way throughout Room 125 at Cleveland Preparatory Technical School.

Author's Note

Natural Nia takes place during the 1970s, which is a period of tremendous change in America. My coming-of-age took place in Oakland, California during that time. It was more than a change of hairstyles, music, and names. Behavior and attitudes shifted. The way the formerly called "Negro" walked in the world began to look different. An air of pride replaced the shame many Black folks had been taught or forced to feel about our NATURAL hair and our sun-kissed skin. When James Brown rhythmically implored us to "Say it Loud I'm Black and I'm Proud" there was no hesitation as we raised clinched fists above our heads. In writing *Natural Nia,* I had the chance to reflect, reminisce, and look ahead. I hope you will do the same.

Get Talking: Discussion Guide

1. Arnetta has experienced a lot of change (the divorce of her parents and her older sister's change of name and hairstyle) in a short amount of time. How do these changes impact how Arnetta sees and feels about herself and the world?

2. What draws Nia to the Black Power Movement?

3. Talk about the similarities and differences in how Brenda and Aunt Ruthie respond to Nia.

4. What do you think about how Mr. Lindsey explains to Arnetta the change going on in the world?

5. The opening line of *Natural Nia* reads, "This is a story about hair." Discuss how this is true and what hair represents to Brenda, Arnetta, and Nia.

6. What does the meeting between Leon, Brenda, and Mr. Randall tell you about the times?

7. Which characters do you find yourself agreeing or disagreeing with most often?

8. Grandma and Aunt Ruthie try to help Arnetta understand everything that is happening. Are they successful? Why? Why not?

9. Compare and contrast the Civil Rights Movement, The Black Power Movement, and the Black Lives Matter Movement.

10. Talk about the relationships between Leon and Brenda, Leon and the children, Brenda and the children, and Arnetta and Nia. How does each relationship help you understand the story?

11. What would you tell Nia and Arnetta about today's Black Lives Matter Movement?

12. What do you think is next for the Graves family?

Natural Nia Playlist

If you enjoyed *Natural Nia,* you'll love these songs from the 1960s and 1970s.

Artist	Song
The Jackson 5	"The Love You Save"
The Staple Singers	"I'll Take You There"
Marvin Gaye	"What's Going On"
James Brown	"Say it Loud I'm Black and I'm Proud"
The Temptations	"Ball of Confusion (That's What the World Is Today)"
The O'Jays	"Love Train"
Al Green	"Let's Stay Together"
Bill Withers	"Lean on Me"
Aretha Franklin	"Rock Steady"
Sly & the Family Stone	"Thank You (Falettinme Be Mice Elf)"
Michael Jackson	"I Wanna Be Where You Are"
Lyn Collins	"Think (About It)"
Stevie Wonder	"Living For the City"
The Spinners	"Could it Be I'm Falling in Love"
Earth, Wind & Fire	"Shining Star"

Edwin Starr	"War"
Gladys Knight & The Pips	"Friendship Train"
Harold Melvin & the Blue Notes	"Wake up Everybody"
The Impressions	"We're A Winner"
The Stylistics	"People Make The World Go Round"

Reading List that Informed the Writing of *Natural Nia*

Angelou, Maya - *I Know Why The Caged Bird Sings*

Baldwin, James - *I Am Not Your Negro*

Brown, Claude - *Manchild In The Promised Land*

Brown, Elaine - *A Taste of Power: A Black Woman's Story*

Cleaver, Eldridge - *Soul On Ice*

DuBois, W.E. B. - *The Souls of Black Folk*

Ellison, Ralph - *Invisible Man*

Giovanni, Nikki - *Ego-Tripping and other Poems for Young People*

Haley, Alex – *Roots: The Saga of an American Family*

Hughes, Langston - *The Ways of White Folks*

Hurston, Zora Neale - *Their Eyes Were Watching God*

Jackson, George - *Soledad Brother: The Prison Letters of George Jackson*

Johnson, James Weldon - *The Autobiography of An Ex-Colored Man*

King Jr., Martin Luther - *Where Do We Go From Here: Chaos of Community?*

Morrison, Toni - *The Bluest Eye*

Moore, Joe Louis - *The Legacy of the Panthers: A Photographic Exhibition, Project of the Dr. Huey P. Newton Foundation*

Muhammad, Elijah - *Message to the Blackman in America*

Shakur, Assata - *Assata: An Autobiography*

Washington, Booker T. - *Up From Slavery*

Wright, Richard - *Native Son*

X, Malcolm - *The Autobiography of Malcolm X: As Told to Alex Haley*

About the Author

At the urging of her friend and mentor, Blanche Richardson, La Rhonda attended Tina McElroy Ansa's first Sea Island Writers' Retreat on Sapelo Island in 2004. It was there where she began to "see" herself as a writer. La Rhonda has contributed to several anthologies and written a serial novel *Jubilee's Journey* and a full-length novel *Unveiled*.

La Rhonda is a native Californian who lives in the San Francisco Bay Area with her husband and biggest fan, Ernest Johnson.

To contact La Rhonda, visit her via social media.

- Twitter: @LaRhondasBooks
- Email: larhondawrites@gmail.com